PeeWee & Plush

*for Mrs. Early's
second grade class,
Have fun with
PeeWee & Plush.*

Johanna Hurwitz

January 2003

PeeWee & Plush

· A Park Pals Adventure ·

Johanna Hurwitz

ILLUSTRATED BY

Patience Brewster

SeaStar Books
NEW YORK

SEASTAR BOOKS
A division of NORTH-SOUTH BOOKS INC.

First published in the United States in 2002 by SeaStar Books,
a division of North-South Books Inc., New York. Published simultaneously in
Canada, Australia, and New Zealand by North-South Books,
an imprint of Nord-Süd Verlag AG, Gossau Zürich, Switzerland.

Library of Congress Cataloging-in-Publication Data
Hurwitz, Johanna.
PeeWee & Plush / Johanna Hurwitz; illustrated by Patience Brewster.
p. cm.
"A park pals adventure."
Summary: PeeWee the guinea pig and his friend Lexi the squirrel help
a new guinea pig adjust to life in the wilds of New York City's Central Park,
but are unsure what to do about the approach of winter.
[1. Guinea pigs—Fiction. 2. Squirrels—Fiction. 3. Winter—Fiction. 4. Central Park
(New York, N.Y.)—Fiction.] I. Title: PeeWee & Plush. II. Brewster, Patience, ill. III. Title.
PZ7.H9574 Pe 2002   [Fic]—dc21   2002002509

The artwork for this book was prepared by using pencil.

ISBN 1-58717-191-0 (reinforced trade edition)
1 3 5 7 9 RTE 10 8 6 4 2

Printed in U.S.A.

For more information about our books, and the authors and artists who create them,
visit our web site: www.northsouth.com

CONTENTS

PeeWee & Plush

CHAPTER ONE

Here Is Plush

My name is PeeWee and I'm a guinea pig. In
my life I've had three homes, two friends,
and one wish.

My first home was the cage in Casey's Pet
Shop, where I was born in a small but cozy
cage. One by one, my four brothers and sisters were adopted by happy, eager children.
My turn came too. At my second home, I
was the pet of a boy named Robbie Fischler.

But one evening I was taken from him and set loose in Central Park. At first it seemed I might not survive at all. For all its beauty and space, the park is full of unexpected dangers for a guinea pig. But gradually I learned how to manage.

Now I live in my third home. It's a hole in the base of a tree. Sometimes it's damp and sometimes it's dusty. But this new home of mine is the best of all, because I've come to love the park and the freedom I have here.

One of my friends is Lexington, a clever and helpful squirrel, who taught me how to find food, shelter, and safety. He's shared his advice and his meals with me and has entertained me with his acrobatic tricks and wise sayings. Lexington told me to call him *Lexi* for short. But I hope to call him that not for short, but for a long, long time.

My other friend was a kind and gentle human being who came to the park because he was lost. My human friend guessed that one guinea pig needs another, just as an eye needs an eyelid and a tongue needs a mouth. So before he left, he brought another guinea pig to the park. It was love at first sight for me. From the moment I saw her, I was struck by Plush's golden brown coat and dark eyes. She was beautiful!

And what's my only wish? I want a family. I watch Lexi as he leaps across the grass or through the trees. Everywhere he's greeted by dozens of cousins, scores of brothers and sisters, and hundreds of aunts and uncles. He pretends that he doesn't care about them. "Squirrels aren't interested in family," he insists. "What good are all those relatives? *Only a nut can fill you up.*" He doesn't seem to take into account that many of the nuts he digs up were buried in the ground by some of those very relatives he thinks are of no importance.

Now that Plush is here in the park with me, my wish can become a reality. In another moon, I'll be six months old. Although a human is still an infant at that age, guinea pigs grow very quickly. A six-month-old guinea pig is an adult. I'm hopeful that before the summer is out, Plush might be interested in starting a family of our own. We'll start small, but who knows? Perhaps someday there will be as many guinea pigs running through the park as there are squirrels.

We may not be able to climb trees. We don't have strong claws and teeth sharp enough to defend ourselves from enemies. But the first guinea pigs weren't born in cages. They lived outdoors in nature. And it can happen again. Maybe Plush and I will begin the rise of a new era in guinea pig history!

☆   ☆   ☆

I'll never forget that first evening when Plush

cuddled up inside my tree hole home. Lexi had presented us with a soft woolen scarf that had lined his nest. Now it was on the floor of my home. Plush pulled it around herself to protect her from the hole's damp chill. I'd become used to it, but it was good that Plush had this extra comfort on her first night in new surroundings.

"There's so much to see and do here," I whispered to her. "Tomorrow I'll show you a whole new world."

"It seems so big. Too big," said Plush softly.

I knew how she felt. It wasn't so long ago when the vastness of the park overwhelmed me too. But now I felt perfectly at home here, and I would do all I could to help her learn to love this new place too. "Don't worry. I'll make sure nothing bad happens to you," I promised her.

Together we listened to the sounds of the park at night: the leaves above us rustling in a slight breeze, a cricket calling to another cricket, and far off the sound of city traffic.

"Are you cold?" I asked Plush.

"How can I be cold?" she asked. "I learned in the pet shop that guinea pigs are warm-blooded, like all other mammals," she reminded me. Still, I could feel her body shaking.

"Rest, rest," I cooed. And gradually her shuddering stopped and her body relaxed. After a time, I knew that she was asleep. I was drifting off too, but I forced myself to stay awake a bit longer. It had been a long time since I had smelled the scent of another guinea pig so close to me. I wanted to enjoy it as long as possible.

When I woke the next morning, I thought I'd dreamed that another guinea pig had come to live with me. Then I opened my eyes and I saw Plush. She wasn't a dream. She was real!

Usually I'd leave my hole as soon as I'd awake. But that morning, I lay quietly and waited until I heard Plush stirring.

"Good morning," I greeted her.

"Is it?" she asked, puzzled. It was the first time she had awakened somewhere other than in a cage, and she seemed confused and anxious.

"Of course!" I jumped up and poked my

head out of the tree hole. "The sun is shining and we must find you some breakfast."

"Will you bring something to me here?" Plush asked.

I turned around. "Don't you want to stretch your legs? Don't you want to smell the fresh air? Don't you want to see the world?"

"Not now," she answered. "Not yet."

"Didn't you sleep well?" I asked.

"I just want to rest here. Breakfast in bed would be a real treat," she told me.

"Of course," I responded. I would do anything to make my new companion as happy as I was.

I ran through the shrubbery that grew near our tree and looked up at the neighboring tree where Lexi lived. Sure enough, he was sitting on a limb chewing on something.

"Good morning," I called to him.

"And a good one it is," he called back. "Shall we give Plush a tour of the park this morning?" He raced down the tree trunk with his usual speed. I always marveled at his ability. "Where's Plush?" he asked.

"She's still in the hole. She wants me to bring her something to eat."

"Bring her something? Is she sick?"

"No. Just resting," I said. I didn't think Plush was ill. I wanted to run back and ask her but decided against it. Instead, I'd find her a choice item to eat and her appetite would tell me about her health.

"*Life in a hole is fit only for a mole,*" said Lexi. He has a way of reciting proverbs that he learned from his mother. They are usually quite right, but sometimes they're just annoying. This was one of those times.

Lexi went to the opening of our hole. "Plush! Come on out," he called.

"Good morning," Plush replied. But she did not move.

Three little sparrows flew down to the foot of our tree. "The sun . . . is out . . . today," they sang, each chirping two syllables of their message. Plush looked out at them, staring wide-eyed at these new visitors. But she did not move.

I began to think she would stay in our hole forever. "I think she's afraid of the outside," I whispered to Lexi.

"But she can't stay inside all day long," he said.

"Why not?" I asked miserably. Here I was with a beautiful mate, and I couldn't convince her to share the world with me.

"She'll starve," said Lexi firmly. "If you don't bring her food, that is."

"I can't do that," I moaned.

"Yes, you can," said Lexi firmly. But he was wrong. I couldn't do it. I spent the next few hours running back and forth bringing new seeds and nuts to Plush. I was tired and miserable and not getting any closer to getting Plush out of the hole. Nevertheless, we had forgotten what goes along with eating: drinking. By midmorning Plush was very thirsty.

"I need a drink," she gasped.

"Water is not like a nut," I explained to her. "I can't carry any to you." I didn't tell her that I could probably find a wet leaf and that might satisfy her need. I saw this as my only chance.

"Come with me," I coaxed. "I know where there is a large puddle nearby. No one will see you. You'll be safe. And you can have a long cool drink."

And so, after great hesitation, Plush pushed her head out of our hole. At last she was outside. Together, we went toward a nearby puddle.

"It's all so big," Plush marveled, looking around as we walked. "How will we ever find our way home again?"

"That's not a problem," I reassured her. The only problem was how would I keep Plush from wanting to go back to our hole to hide again?

CHAPTER TWO

Plush Gets Angry

Plush stuck her face down into the puddle and eagerly lapped up water. Now that she was outside in the sunlight, I could admire her sleek, golden brown coat and dark eyes much better than I could inside our hole.

When she finally satisfied her thirst, she turned and looked around. "So this is the park," she said. Did I hear a bit of curiosity in her voice?

"I never knew the world was so big," she said, looking up at the tall trees around us and then across toward the playground.

"This is just a tiny corner of the park," I told her. "It goes on and on, bigger than a thousand cages, bigger than a hundred pet shops, bigger than dozens of city streets. There's a huge lake and several smaller ponds, a great lawn, statues to admire and trees to shade us. There's a carousel for children to ride on and a big zoo filled with many more animals than you ever saw in the pet shop." I stopped for breath. Lexi says that not one of his relatives is as enthusiastic about the wonders of the park as I am.

"The park smells different from the pet

shop," commented Plush, sniffing the air. "It's better," she admitted.

Those were her first words of praise about the park.

"And what about the food here? Didn't you enjoy your breakfast this morning?" I wanted to know.

Plush nodded. "It's the bigness of it all," she explained. "That's what scares me. My mother told me that I was going to live in a small cage all my life. Not in a big space like this."

"You're right," I told her. "The park *is* big. But we're much bigger than many of its inhabitants. Let me show you," I said, leading her into a nearby bush. "Sit still and watch the ground," I instructed.

Plush held her body still and only twitched her face muscles a couple of times. "What are we looking for?" she asked, puzzled.

"Look at your right foot," I said.

Plush looked down. A pair of ants, each carrying the smallest crumb of bread, walked past her foot and toward their hole.

"This park is full of animals," I told Plush. "Many are bigger than us, many are faster, and many are stronger. Some can do all sorts of things that we've never dreamed of doing," I said, thinking of the flying birds. "But we are much, much bigger than the millions of insects who live here. Some are so small, you'll never see them. And some of the animals are so big, they'll never notice us." I was thinking of the horses that I'd seen trotting along their special trails.

"Follow me." I motioned to Plush. We moved out from under the bush. "Now look up."

Plush did as I asked. We could both see the birds that circled the trees around us. "Some of those birds are half your size," I told her.

"I wouldn't want to fly like that," Plush said. "I feel dizzy just watching them."

She looked down at the ground again. "Oh, what's that? It looks delicious," Plush said, moving quickly toward a nearby flower. "I think I'll have a bite."

"It's a buttercup," I told her. "It looks pretty but don't be fooled. Buttercups are poisonous to eat."

"How do you know?" Plush asked. She already had the bright yellow flower in her mouth and was biting into it.

Acting fast, I lunged forward to grab the buttercup from her with my teeth. Somehow, I missed—and bit Plush by mistake. The flower fell out of her mouth as she squealed with pain.

I felt terrible. Never in a hundred moons would I have wanted to hurt her.

"I'm sorry," I started to say. But even before the words were out of my mouth,

Plush darted off. I thought she'd only go a few paws away. She'd be too frightened to go too far. But to my horror, she scampered in and out of the shrubbery. Suddenly I was in a panic. From one moment to the next, I'd lost sight of her. Where had she gone?

CHAPTER THREE

Looking for Plush

It didn't make sense. An hour ago, Plush was afraid to leave the safety of my hole. Then, finally, I'd gotten her to go outside. And now she'd run off into the unknown, which had so terrified her.

I've come to know the park as a wonderful place. But I also knew that there were dangers awaiting a small animal who wasn't careful. I had to find Plush before she came to harm. As simple a thing as nibbling on another buttercup could mean disaster.

How would Plush know that guinea pigs must never eat fool's parsley, wood anemones, lily of the valley, bindweeds, thorn apples, foxglove, larkspur, bleeding heart, horsetails, water parsnip, henbane, rhubarb, and ragwort? I'd never heard of any of those odd names until I came to the park. Mostly I learned from my own stomach after eating those plants. Other things I learned from Lexi's warnings.

As I pushed my way through the under-brush looking for Plush, I had even more worries. The park is filled with dangerous skaters, bicycles, and speeding cars. And what about dogs running through the park to get exercise? Even though signs say dogs must be kept on leashes, sometimes their owners don't pay attention. More than once a dog has almost chewed me to bits! And if one of the many children, parents, or park attendants who are around made a grab for Plush, I'd probably never see her again.

From time to time I stopped to catch my breath, to listen for sounds, and to sniff for her scent. Finally, I caught a familiar whiff, but just then, I also heard a sound I knew too well. A park attendant was sitting on one of the peculiar motor carts that cut the grass. I'd learned to keep clear of those dangerous vehicles. It could slice off my leg as it was clipping the grass. I followed Plush's scent toward the ever-louder sound. Would she know enough to keep out of its path?

I ran toward the closest bush and heard

a voice calling my name. It was Lexi. "Here I am," I called, sticking my head out from under the shrubbery.

He dashed under the bush with me. "I was looking for you," he said. "And where is Plush? Is she still inside your hole?"

"I wish she were," I shouted out over the noise of the grass-cutter. I told him the events of the past half hour. I even told Lexi how I had accidentally bitten Plush. "I didn't mean to do it," I told him. "But I had to make her spit out that buttercup."

Lexi nodded. "I know, I know," he said. "*Better an empty mouth than a stomach full of pain.*"

Lexi may have said something more, but his words were completely drowned out by the loud roar of the cutting machine. I shuddered both from the sound and the thought that poor Plush might be under its blade.

As the machine moved away and its sound diminished, Lexi said, "Wait here. I can run faster. I'll find Plush for you."

He scooted out from under the bush and I remained watching from beneath its branches as he ran. If anyone would find Plush quickly, it was Lexi. It felt good now to rest in the shade of the bush. I was worried about Plush, but I was tired too. I'd spent a lot of energy that morning finding the choicest tidbits for her to eat. I drifted off in an uneasy sleep.

The next thing I knew, I heard Lexi's voice again.

"Wake up, sleepyhead. I've found the lost Plush."

I rubbed my eyes. What a relief it was to see Plush standing in front of me, safe and sound!

"I wasn't lost," Plush said, sounding irritated. "I knew exactly where I was."

"And where was that?" asked Lexi.

"In Central Park, in New York City."

"True enough," said Lexi. "But could you have found your way back to PeeWee's hole again?"

"Why would I want to go back there?" Plush asked. "First he bit me. And then he let you come looking for me while he took a nap."

"Just a minute," I protested. "I *was* looking for you until Lexi took over. And I didn't mean to bite you. Honest. Please forgive me," I begged Plush.

"I'll think about it," she responded.

"How long will it take?" I wanted to know.

"Stop quarreling," scolded Lexi. "I just saw something delicious to eat. Save your mouths for food and not for angry words." He ran out from the bush and returned a minute later dragging a round piece of bread with a hole in the middle that had been dropped by a careless human.

"Who gets the hole?" asked Lexi as we all began to nibble on this tasty find.

"Help yourself. It's all yours," said Plush.

That was the first time I'd heard her make a joke. There was so much about her personality that I had yet to learn. But I guess she had much to learn about me. One can't become the best of friends in just a few hours. Even Lexi and I needed a bit of time to get to really know and appreciate each other.

As far as I knew, Plush and I were the only guinea pigs in all of Central Park. We had to trust and understand each other. Otherwise, how could we have a family together someday?

CHAPTER FOUR

A Night at the Opera

One good thing came from my biting Plush. She wasn't eager to return to my hole with me. After a morning of trying to get her out into the park, I discovered that now I couldn't get her back into my cozy hideaway.

"Show me the park," Plush said to Lexi after we finished eating. It stung that she didn't ask me.

"Not now. *An afternoon rest is always best!*"

Lexi told Plush. It was another of his mother's sayings.

"I'll rest tonight," Plush said. "If you don't want to show me the park, I'll just make my own discoveries."

I looked at Lexi with alarm. Now that he had found her, we couldn't possibly let her out of our sight.

"Come along," said Lexi good-naturedly. He led the way, and Plush and I followed. "We'll go to Turtle Pond," he said, turning and winking at me. Turtle Pond was quite a distance away. Lexi's wink told me he planned to tire Plush out so we could all stop and take a rest en route.

"Turtle Pond?" said Plush eagerly. "There were several turtles in the pet shop where I used to live."

"I've never seen a turtle here," said Lexi. "It's just a name, not a creature."

"Too bad," said Plush. "Turtles are quite wise and very gentle, unlike some animals I can name. I enjoyed speaking with those in the shop."

Was that a crack at me? I couldn't tell.

We walked from one bit of protected shrubbery to another. "It's important not to be seen by humans," Lexi instructed Plush.

"Why? In the pet shop I saw dozens of humans every day. It was a human who cleaned my cage and fed me. Humans were always good to me and none ever hurt me," she said.

Was that another crack?

"These humans will be surprised to see a

guinea pig in the park. They'll want to catch you and take you away to their home," Lexi explained patiently.

"Is that bad?" asked Plush. "All guinea pigs want a warm, clean, safe home."

She's saying my hole is damp and dirty, I thought. How could I have lost her trust so quickly? I felt miserable.

Just then a child's rubber ball came flying through the air and landed inches away from us. We all froze in our spots. Then clever Lexi ran around in a circle near the ball while I pushed Plush under a thick hedge. A moment later two small children, followed by an adult, came to retrieve the ball. We kept still until they turned away.

"I hope I didn't hurt you," I said to Plush. "I wanted to help you hide quickly."

"Just keep your paws off me," she said coolly. "I can hide or not hide as I choose."

I sighed. To think this day had begun with such joy. Now it was turning into a nightmare.

We walked on toward Turtle Pond. I knew our slow pace was frustrating for Lexi. From time to time he would rush up a tree and greet a cousin or two on a high branch. Then he would make a huge leap and return to us.

"How much farther?" asked Plush.

"We're halfway there," said Lexi. "Do you want to rest for a bit?" he asked hopefully.

"No," Plush said firmly. But her small steps grew even smaller as we continued.

To get to Turtle Pond we had to cross a

wide road built for cars traveling through the park. "Keep to the edge under the leaves," Lexi told Plush. "I'll tell you when it's safe to cross."

Squirrels are lucky enough to have two choices. They can run quickly across the road, or they can jump above it on tree limbs. But it's *never* safe for a guinea pig to cross a road. We have to wait until there's no traffic and then move as fast as we can. That's why I usually only cross the road very, very early in the morning or very, very late at night when the fewest cars are driving through the park.

Lexi climbed a tree to get a better view. "Wait till I tell you to go," he called down to us. Plush and I stood ready at the edge of the road and hid in some tall grass. Suddenly Lexi called out, "Now! Go for it!"

Plush and I raced as fast as we could. We had just made it to the other side when I heard the sound of car tires whizzing past. It would be so easy for us to be beneath them. But thankfully, we weren't. We lay on the grass panting for breath.

"We did it!" I said to Plush. "That was good running you did."

"Thanks," she said. And for the first time that day I felt as if we were a team.

"Ready?" Lexi called to us.

I looked at Plush. She seemed exhausted, but I knew she was too proud to admit it.

We were very close to Turtle Pond, but I didn't think she could make it. "I need a break," I shouted to my squirrel friend. "Let's rest here for a few minutes."

Nearby there was a deep shrub and I urged Plush to hide in its shaded safety with me. She came willingly enough but still made a point of settling down as far away from me as possible. It was better than nothing, I thought.

Lexi stuck his nose under the shrub. "I'll be back in a while," he said. "Now you know why squirrels like to travel alone."

By the time Lexi returned, Plush and I felt refreshed by a long nap. The sun was moving westward in the sky, and we could see the feet and legs of many people walking across the area. There seemed to be hundreds and hundreds of people all heading in the same direction.

"What's going on?" I asked Lexi. In my weeks in the park, I had learned a lot. But there was still so much I didn't know. I'd seen Sunday crowds before, but I'd never seen this many people so late in the day.

"There's an activity tonight over on the Great Lawn," Lexi reported. "I don't know what it is but all these people carrying so many blankets and bags can only mean one thing: garbage. We'll certainly have a wonderful feast when they all go home."

"But what can we eat now?" asked Plush. "In the pet shop I could eat pellets whenever I wanted. They might not taste as good as the food here in the park, but they were always available."

"No problem," said Lexi. He ran off and within a minute came back holding a couple of seeds. *"Dig, dig, and you'll find something big,"* he told us. These seeds weren't exactly big, but Lexi came back several times with more. They were crunchy like pet shop pellets, but their taste was much more delicious. I looked over at Plush. Her fur was a little disheveled from sleeping in the dirt, but she was still the most beautiful guinea pig in the world.

Rested and full of food, we sat together talking. Lexi told Plush stories about the park. He told her about how we had become friends and said many fine things about me. She seemed especially impressed when Lexi told her that I was the only animal in the entire park who knew how to read. On another day I might have felt embarrassed hearing so much praise, but now I was glad. I needed all the help I could get to regain Plush's trust and win her affection. And from time to time, I noticed her looking at me with renewed interest.

The sky was still quite light when we began to hear a sound that was unusual in the park. There was human music playing very loudly nearby.

"Oh my heavens!" shrieked Plush, suddenly looking very alert. "That's the overture to *Tosca*."

"What's that?" I asked.

"*Tosca*. It's an opera by Giacomo Puccini. It's one of my favorites. I love everything by him: *Tosca*, *La Bohème*, *Madama Butterfly*. . . . They're all so beautiful."

Lexi and I looked at each other, puzzled. I'd heard music coming from the boom boxes that some of the people carried in the park, but I'd never heard it so loud and it never sounded like this. Personally, I prefer birdsong to human music.

"Mr. Josephi, who owned the pet shop where I used to live, always had the radio on," Plush explained to us. "He especially loved to listen to opera. I've heard many of them in his store."

"Would you like to *see* the opera?" I asked Plush.

"You mean we could actually do that?" she asked incredulously.

"It's just a short walk from here to the Great Lawn. That's where the performance must be."

And so that's why we didn't go to Turtle Pond, and it's how I got to see my first opera. There were men and women wearing long outfits that looked incredibly uncomfortable to me, singing in voices that were unnaturally loud. Although I could hear

them perfectly well, I couldn't make out a single word. Whenever the singing stopped, the hundreds of people sitting on blankets or folding chairs would break into loud applause. Plush tapped her paws together in delight too.

"Why can't I understand them?" I asked Plush.

"They're singing in Italian, silly," she told me.

"Do you understand Italian?" I asked in amazement.

"No," she admitted. "You don't have to understand all the words to enjoy an opera. You can feel the emotion in the music. Imagine! I'm hearing a live performance of *Tosca* here in the park," Plush said happily. "Who could believe it? I only wish Mr.

Josephi were here too. He would be so delighted."

"Maybe he is," I wondered aloud. I'd never seen so many humans before in my life. There were hundreds of them.

"Oh, what a good thought," said Plush, looking at me. "You're right. Perhaps Mr. Josephi is out there somewhere."

As we sat under a shrub, I saw sheets of green paper with words printed on them on the ground around us. With everyone concentrating on the scene before them, I dared to venture out and grab one with my teeth. Then sitting back under the bush, I studied it. Plush was so involved with the opera performance that she didn't notice me poring over the green page. From it, I learned the names of all the singers and all of the people who had sponsored this event.

Much later, when the opera was over and the audience had left, the sky was dark. Only a few park lights and the moon above cast any light on the Great Lawn.

"Now we can feast," said Lexi. "The park personnel will be cleaning up early tomorrow morning, so this is our chance."

Plush ate her first grape and a wheat cracker. I had a piece of peach and some salted peanuts. Lexi kept busy eating and hiding food in holes that he dug all around the field. Many of his relatives snatched up food that had been dropped by the humans too. Not far from us, I saw Lexi's fat old uncle Ninety-nine munching on a piece of cookie. I even noticed an old acquaintance, a raccoon named Sewer Drain, busy devouring a sandwich which had been left behind. There was plenty for all of us.

"Why do you make holes and bury food?" Plush asked Lexi.

"I can't eat it all," Lexi said, "and I hope by burying some of it that I'll be able to find it later in the year when winter comes and there are no nuts and seeds and leaves available."

"What is winter?" Plush asked.

"It's many moons away from now. But when it comes, the days are short, the nights are long, the air is cold, the ground is hard, and life is harder."

I shuddered at Lexi's words. But on such a warm, moonlit summer night, it was hard to imagine a time called winter. So I turned my attention back to the food in front of me.

When we had eaten as much as we could possibly manage, it was too late to begin the long trek back to our homes. "Let's spend the night right here," suggested Lexi, and both Plush and I agreed.

Lexi climbed up the nearest tree. Plush crawled under a nearby bush. She was making a funny sound in her throat. It took me a moment to realize that she was trying to hum one of the melodies from the opera. I crawled in beside her.

"I have some good news for you," I whispered in the darkness when she stopped humming.

"What is it?" she asked. Her voice no longer held the anger of the afternoon. Where had I read the words *music soothes the savage beast*? Guinea pigs aren't savage, but all animals get angry sometimes. And the opera had worked its magic on Plush.

"I saw on the program that a different opera will be performed here later in the summer. It's called *La Traviata*. Have you ever heard of it?"

"*La Traviata*? That's another wonderful opera. It's by Giuseppe Verdi," exclaimed Plush. "Oh, it would be amazing to have a second experience like tonight. Will you come with me?" she asked.

I wanted to jump for joy. I knew I was forgiven. Thank you, Giacomo Puccini, wherever you are!

CHAPTER FIVE

What Is Winter?

That began a very happy time for me. Each day Plush and I grew to know each other better. I learned which seeds and leaves were her favorites and saved them for her. Plush was eager to learn more about park life and asked me a hundred questions a day. Best of all, we played together in the tall grasses that grew all around us.

It had always been impossible for me

to join in Lexi's games of tag, chase, and hide-and-seek that he played with all of his siblings and cousins. I couldn't keep up with squirrel speed and I couldn't climb trees or jump from limb to limb. But Plush and I were evenly matched for playing games. We hid in the grass or in small crevices in the earth or under rocks. We chased each other at our slower guinea pig pace and tickled each other with long flower stems and grasses. Each day brought new pleasures.

There were surprises too. It didn't rain until Plush had been living in the park for ten days.

"What is this leaking from the sky?" she asked in alarm when she stuck her head outside. She had never seen rain before.

"Rain? Is that another name for water?" she asked.

"It's water from above. It won't last long. Perhaps a few hours. Perhaps all day."

Plush walked outside and took a morning drink from a nearby puddle. "I don't like it," she informed me. "I like water to hold still so I can drink it. I don't want it falling on my head."

"Then stay inside," I told her.

"But what can we do? There's no room for any of our games in here."

I knew how we could spend our time. Until now there hadn't been an opportunity to show off my reading. My mother had taught me from the paper scraps that lined our cage in the pet shop. And thanks to Lexi, I own a collection of small books that have been left behind by people who visit the park. So Plush and I passed many pleasant hours in my hole as I read poems from one of my books.

"Read that again," Plush asked after I finished one of them.

> *"The north wind doth blow,*
> *And we shall have snow,*
> *And what will poor robin do then,*
> *Poor thing?*
> *He'll sit in a barn,*
> *To keep himself warm,*
> *And hide his head under his wing,*
> *Poor thing!"*

"That's a very sad poem," said Plush. "And I don't understand all the words either."

I didn't understand all of the rhyme myself. I knew about robins, but *barn*? *snow*? These were words I didn't know. But I had a feeling that it had something to do with what Lexi had told us about winter. Wasn't that a time of snow?

Later, while Plush was napping, I found another puzzling poem. I read it slowly. It was called "No" and the poet was Thomas Hood.

No sun—no moon!
No morn—no noon!
No dawn—no dusk—
  no proper time of day—
No sky—no earthly view—
No distance looking blue—

I shuddered at these words. It sounded like the end of time. I breathed deeply and tried to be brave as I went on. But the words seemed to bring more and more gloom. And finally the poem concluded:

No warmth, no cheerfulness, no
  healthful ease,
No comfortable feel in any member—
No shade, no shine, no butterflies,
  no bees,

No fruits, no flowers, no leave[s]
    no birds,
November!

next

Where had I heard that word before? November? I said it over and over to myself trying to remember and then suddenly I knew. Back when I was a young guinea pig and my mother was teaching me how to read, she had also taught me some of the rhymes and songs that she knew. One of them was about the months: *Thirty days hath September, April, June, and November. . . .* November occurred during one of the moons and from the words in Thomas Hood's poem, I could guess it was not his favorite time of the year. I guessed it would not be mine either.

Later that day the rain stopped and the

day was another bright and sunny one. . forgot my fears once again. But it wasn't for long. A couple of days later, Lexi dragged a heavy magazine over to our hole.

"A woman left this," he told me. "There're lots of black squiggles in here for you."

Squiggles are what Lexi calls words. I've tried teaching him how to read, but he is far too restless to sit still long enough to master even a single letter of the alphabet. Plush, on the other hand, who quickly learned all of the uppercase letters, was eager to learn more.

I went under a bush to study this new piece of literature. The information inside was not of much interest: mostly about cosmetics (that funny red coloring that human women put on their lips and

the black that surrounds their eyes), and how
to lose weight (why would an animal want to
do that?). There were lots of terrible pictures
in the magazine too. I saw page after page of
women wearing long coats or jackets made
out of animal pelts. I shuddered at the
thought, even though I knew guinea
pigs are so small that no human would ever

attempt to take our skins to make a piece of clothing.

But then something else in these pictures caught my attention. They were all well covered. There were woolen scarves, like the one that Plush and I had on the floor of our home, covering their throats. The people even had coverings on their hands and sturdy-looking shoes on their feet. But most significant of all, the people were standing on mounds of something white. There were piles of the white stuff all around them. It looked just like clouds, but whoever heard of clouds on the ground?

Plush looked over my shoulder. She pointed to a letter *P* and identified it. Then she laughed. "What strange pictures," she said.

"Yes," I agreed. "I wonder if Lexi ever saw anything like this before?"

Later that morning when Lexi came by, I had a chance to ask. "What does this picture mean?" I inquired.

Lexi jumped right into the middle of the magazine page. "Snow!" he announced. "Those pictures show you what winter looks like."

"You mean the clouds come onto the ground in winter?" I asked, puzzled.

"Not clouds," he said. "First, tiny white flakes come from the sky. Then more and more. They settle on the ground and pile up on top of one another. Before you know it there can be several inches or even more."

"It looks pretty," observed Plush.

"Pretty, yes," agreed Lexi. "But also cold. Snow is very, very cold."

"That's just like the poem," exclaimed Plush. And then together we recited the words "*The north wind doth blow, / And we shall have snow.*"

After a pause, I asked Lexi another question, although I was afraid I knew the answer. "When does winter begin. When does it snow?" I asked.

"Here in the park, we begin to feel the pinch and pain of winter when it is the Beaver Moon. I believe humans call that time November."

It was just as I'd feared.

"Winter sounds terrible," said Plush. "Will it be here soon?"

"It always comes sooner than we want it,"

said Lexi. "But there are many moons until it arrives."

I moved over to Plush and rubbed against her. "Don't worry about winter," I said to her. "We'll make a plan and the winter will not harm us."

"Yes, we'll put our heads together and think of something," she agreed.

I worried that it would take more than our two small heads to come up with one good plan.

CHAPTER SIX

A Trip to the Zoo

The weather was beautiful. The park was lush and green and filled with wonderful things to eat. Plush and I grew closer than ever. Every day was full of fun and yet, I was not completely happy. The poem by Thomas Hood and Lexi's description of winter began to haunt me. I thought about that coming season when I lay in my hole in the dark of the night.

No sun—no moon!
No morn—no noon!

How those words made me shiver. I thought of them whenever a cloud hid the sun during the day. I knew there was no way to prevent winter from coming. But I didn't have a plan to protect Plush and me when the cold months arrived.

I turned to Lexi for advice. He'd lived in the park his entire life and had already survived the snow. "What can we do to get through the winter?" I asked him.

"That's a good question." He scratched himself thoughtfully. "All creatures have a winter plan, but what is the guinea pig's plan? I don't think you can play in the snow like us squirrels. And a deep snowfall could cover the entrance to your hole. You might not be able to dig your way out for days. Especially if the snow turns to ice."

"Ice?" I said, and a shiver went through my body. Why was it winter was filled with so many things I'd never known about? "What do other creatures do?" I asked.

"Many birds fly south," said Lexi. "That's their plan. It's a long way to go. I'm glad to stay right here."

I didn't know where south was. "How far away is south?" I asked.

"Farther than even I could get if I ran for days and days," Lexi replied.

Oh no, I thought to myself. What would take Lexi days of running would take Plush and me forever. "Is there anything else you can suggest?" I asked him.

"You could always hibernate," he said.

"Hibernate? What's that?"

"Sleep," said Lexi. "Some warm-blooded animals go into a long sleep during the cold weather. They live off the fat in their bodies until spring comes. You could always do that."

Sleep through all the moons of winter? It sounded very boring to me. I didn't think I would like that at all. And I wasn't sure Plush would want to do that either.

"Oh, well, don't worry about that now," said Lexi. "Enjoy the summer moons while they're here."

If only it was that easy. Plush seemed to think everything would work out because she began talking to me about raising a family here in the park. I knew this meant that she truly had grown to care for me and to trust me if she was willing to accept me as her mate. It showed she thought I'd be able to care for her and our babies. If only I could feel confident that this was true.

It takes about seventy days for baby guinea pigs to grow inside the mother. Right now we were late in the period animals referred to as Thunder Moon, but humans called July. So we couldn't expect to become parents until the Hunter's Moon, which is mid-October. Well, we couldn't just sit around thinking about it. So we kept busy to pass the time.

I suggested to Plush that we go and visit the zoo. I thought of it first as a place where Plush had never been before. But then it occurred to me that while we were there,

I might learn how other animals survive through the winter.

I called up to Lexi and invited him to join us in our expedition.

"Maybe I'll meet you there later," he called down to me from his perch.

That made sense. He preferred to travel at his own speed. After all, he could make the trip to the zoo in a quarter of the time it would take Plush and me to get there.

We started out at dawn the next day. The zoo is located in the southern end of the park, in the opposite direction from the Great Lawn. To get there we had to travel quite a distance. The entire park is a great lawn to creatures as small as Plush and me. Still, I had told her a lot about what to expect, and Plush was eager to make the trip.

"I thought I saw all the animals in the world when I lived in the pet shop," she told me.

"You didn't see any squirrels there," I reminded her.

"That's true. But there were turtles and cats, dogs of all sizes, many birds, mice, gerbils, hamsters, fish," she listed for me.

"But you never saw a bear, did you? Or a sea lion?"

"What are they like?" asked Plush.

"Bigger than the biggest dog you ever saw; as big as the horses we saw last week that were trotting through the park," I told her.

"How could a cage be that big?" asked Plush. She was thinking of her cage home in the pet shop, which was very small.

"Cages come in all sizes," I informed her.

The zoo opens every day at ten in the morning. It closes at five. One of the advantages of being a guinea pig was that we could enter and leave when we wished. We weren't limited to human hours. We didn't have to wait in line or buy a ticket either!

At the entrance to the zoo there is a big sign: **Central Park Wildlife Center— Black Tie Optional.** Underneath the words was a picture of an

animal that I recognized from my previous visits to the zoo. It was a penguin.

"What does that sign say?" Plush asked me after she tried unsuccessfully to read it for herself.

I didn't understand what the words **Black Tie Optional** meant, but since Plush couldn't correct me, I guessed. "It says, 'All are welcome.' That's why it's so crowded here," I explained.

There were many groups of children accompanied by adults. They were all so busy looking at animals inside the cages that no one noticed a pair of small animals at their feet. Nevertheless, Plush and I took care to spend most of our time hidden behind bushes or in shady corners where we weren't noticed.

We arrived just before 11:30 A.M., which is when the zookeepers feed the three sea lions: Scooter, April, and Seaweed. They caught the small fish that were thrown to them and swallowed them whole. The children and adults applauded when one of the sea lions made a catch. But Plush and I agreed that we wouldn't be so happy swallowing *our* food whole. In the first place, guinea pigs need to bite and chew to keep their teeth from getting too long. And what about taste? If you swallowed everything whole you'd never be able to taste anything at all!

I kept busy reading all the signs aloud to Plush. I was proud to show off my talent. "Snow monkeys live in troops of ten to eight hundred" I read aloud, although I could only see three inside the cage.

They were busy scratching themselves.

"That's just like Lexi and his squirrel relatives," Plush pointed out. I'm not sure if she was referring to the scratching or the large family unit.

We moved on. There was lots of shrubbery in the zoo, so we always felt protected. Plush was stunned by the size of the giant polar bears. "They are the largest land-based carnivores in the world," I told her.

"What are carnivores?" asked Plush.

"Meat eaters."

"Are we meat?" she asked anxiously.

"No," I told her. "We're guinea pigs, we're rodents, we're mammals, but we're not meat." It was a lie. Of course we're meat, but what was the sense in alarming her? I read aloud the list of foods that polar bears eat: ". . . mice, lemmings, hares, waterfowl, seabirds and their eggs, mussels, fish, carrion. . . ."

"Oh, you're right. The list doesn't say guinea pigs," said Plush with relief, "though a nearsighted polar bear might mistake us for hairy mice."

"In nature, polar bears live in very cold climates where guinea pigs would never exist. Only in a large zoo like this one can you find such a range of diverse animals from different climates," I pointed out. "Besides there are thick glass walls between us and the bears."

Plush kicked the glass wall in front of her with one of her front feet. Nothing happened. "You're right," she said. "We're safe out here."

I heard parents pointing out to their children that there were blocks of ice in the polar bear enclosure. "They don't like hot summer days like this," a father said.

It was only then that it occurred to me that none of the zoo animals had to worry about the coming of winter. If the zoo arranged to keep polar bears cool in warm weather, certainly the opposite would be done too. Animals that couldn't survive in winter's snow would have heated cages when the weather became cold. I stood looking at the polar bears and felt miserable. I'd been so hoping that I could learn something at the zoo that would help Plush and me.

Plush was so busy looking at everything that she was unaware that my mood had changed. She ran from area to area and I followed close behind. She wanted to see everything. The section of the zoo that most interested Plush was the rain-forest exhibit. We waited until someone pushed the door open and scooted inside. The zookeepers had created an environment that was many degrees warmer than outside. There were colorful birds flying overhead and strange plants that I'd never seen before. Even the rich, earthy smells were new to us. We hid inside a hollow log. It was dark in the log, but I could see Plush's eyes shining brightly.

"PeeWee?" she asked. "Is the zoo open year-round?"

"Yes, it is," I told her. "We can come back whenever you want. You really seem to like it here."

"I do. I do. And I've had a wonderful

thought," she told me. "I remember what Lexi told us about the cold moons of winter that come every year. I also overheard some birds talking. They say snow and ice cover the ground and it's hard to find food. They say some animals freeze in the cold. But if this area is open, we could come and hide in here. No one would know we were here except the animals and birds who live in this rain forest. I'm sure they wouldn't object if we paid them an extended visit."

I looked at her with amazement. "Plush, you're brilliant!" I exclaimed. She was absolutely right. This area could serve as our barn. It was a plan that could help us survive even the worst weather ahead.

The zoo signs said that the rain-forest

occupants came from many places like West Africa, New Guinea, Southeast Asia, and South America. And since once upon a time, all guinea pigs lived in South America, I realized that we'd feel right at home in here. Perhaps the red-crested cardinals and the bay-headed tanagers flying above us, who came from South America, could tell us something about the land of our ancestors.

I think Plush was ready to move into the rain forest right then and there. But it was still summer outside, and so I urged her to follow me to the exit. "Lexi may be looking for us," I reminded her.

Outside, the bright sunlight blinded us briefly. We regained our normal vision just a moment too late for, suddenly, a small

hand snatched Plush right off the ground.

"Mommy, Mommy, look what I found," a child's voice called out.

I didn't know what to do. And before I could think of something, Lexi landed at my feet with a thud. Then he took another leap and jumped onto the shoes of the child who was holding Plush. Startled, the child dropped my companion and ran to her mother.

"Quickly, hide!" I called to Plush. She ran with me into a bush.

"A squirrel jumped on me," we heard the child whining to her mother.

"Don't be silly, sweetie," said the mother. "Squirrels are busy looking for nuts. Come, let's buy some ice cream."

The mother took the child's hand and using her other hand pushed a carriage with a smaller child inside.

"Are you all right?" I asked Plush anxiously.

"Yes, yes," she said. "I was held by many children in the pet shop. But none of them ever dropped me before," she said, licking her sore feet.

Lexi crawled into the bush beside us. "Good timing?" he asked proudly.

"Good timing," I agreed. I hated to think what could have happened if Lexi had not arrived at the very moment that he did.

"Wait here," he told us. "I had my eye on a great treat before I was interrupted by that child."

Plush and I were not in a hurry to leave our safe spot, and so we waited. Two minutes later, Lexi returned dragging a paper bag still half filled with popcorn.

"This will keep us busy," he said.

"You're a great friend, Lexi," I responded gratefully.

Lexi didn't say anything. He couldn't. His mouth was filled with popcorn.

CHAPTER SEVEN

Summer Days

And so our days passed. Most were calm, filled with birdsong and succulent meals. Occasionally there was a moment of panic, like when the child grabbed Plush or when I almost had my leg severed by a toddler on a tricycle who made an unexpected detour through the grass. But the longer we lived in the park, the more clever Plush and I were about keeping our whereabouts hidden from the humans.

We attended *La Traviata*, which appealed to me no more than the first opera. Once again the singers insisted on singing in Italian even though I'm certain most of the audience didn't know a word of that language. But it was worth sitting through the entire opera just to make Plush so happy. And of course there was another sumptuous feast after the event was over.

There were no more operas after that, but signs announced two concerts.

"Music by Beethoven, Mozart, and Schubert. Do you like that?" I said to Plush, reading from a sign. So many unusual names, I thought.

"I enjoy all classical music," she told me.

There were also a couple of performances of Shakespearean plays. I must confess that most of the plays went over my head. But as Lexi was quick to point out, when the plays were over, much went into my head—by way of my mouth. All of these special events in the park meant rich meals for the animal residents.

Plush began to talk more about our future family. Guinea pigs are not much for dancing, but I always danced for joy when she discussed our unborn children.

Lexi was less impressed. "Male squirrels don't get so excited about their offspring," he told me.

"In some species of animals, the fathers

are separated from the babies because they might cause them harm," Plush told me. "I learned about that at the pet shop when they put the male gerbils and male rabbits in separate cages from their offspring."

"I would never hurt our children," I promised Plush.

"I know," she said confidently.

I glowed. It was hard to believe there was a time when she didn't trust me.

August is a wonderful month in the park. There was the lush growth of leaves everywhere providing us with an endless meal. And there were wild raspberries and delicious roots to eat as well. On some days it rained, but that was all right. We had the choice of reading in our cozy hole or playing outside even if it meant getting wet.

The rain was warm, and it cleaned the dust and dirt from our hair. Afterward, back in the hole, we groomed each other.

During those hot days of August, more people than ever used the park. Plush and I had to be more cautious than ever as we moved outside in the grass. And Lexi kept very busy digging hole after hole and burying choice tidbits for the winter. He also stuffed his nest in the tree with additional bits of food and started bringing leaves to line it more completely.

September was a lovely month too. The

evenings were cooler, but not unpleasant. Nuts were ripe and plentiful. Leaves began to change from green to glorious shades of red and yellow. The park was more beautiful than ever.

"Enjoy it while you can," Lexi warned us as Plush and I were jumping in and out of a small pile of fallen leaves. "First the leaves fall. Then the snow falls. Winter is coming."

"Thanks for the reminder," I said.

"I'm glad you have a plan for the winter," Lexi told Plush and me. "It won't be long now. I can feel it in the air."

I had described the inside of the rain forest to him and said how easy it would be for us to hide there. "You can come too," I had invited him. After I made the offer, I had second thoughts. Plush and I knew how to curl up small and remain quiet for long periods of time. Lexi was all dash and dart, jump and jive. It wouldn't take long for him to be discovered in the rain forest. And if the zookeepers found him, they might start looking for other visitors like Plush and me.

"Thanks for the invitation. But I don't want to leave my tree hole," Lexi said. "Still, I'm relieved to know you have a plan," he added.

"It was Plush's idea," I admitted. "She's very clever."

Plush was indeed clever. And now she was also growing very big. Our babies were due before long.

Lexi was with us one afternoon when Plush suddenly gave a little gasp. "I felt them," she said.

"What did you feel?" both Lexi and I asked her.

"Our babies," said Plush. "They're beginning to move inside of me. It won't be long before they are born."

"Hurray!" I shouted. Soon I would become a father. My wish would come true.

CHAPTER EIGHT

Guinea Pig Family

Our offspring, or puppies as guinea pig babies are called, were born just after dawn following the harvest moon. Plush had known the time was near. She woke me and the two of us lay waiting. I had dreamt of this moment for so long, but now that it was here, I was very nervous.

Suddenly, Plush let out a soft groan because she felt a cramp. The cramps hurt, but we knew they wouldn't last long. Still, I wished that there was some way that I could help her. But without any assistance from me, within a short time our first son was born. He was a solid-looking fellow with the same coloring as his mother.

"Pudge," I shouted out. "He's a pudgy little boy and Pudge is a perfect name for him."

"I'll name the next one," said Plush, and a moment later there he was. "Perky!" she said, looking at our second son whose coloring was dark brown, just like mine.

"Do you think there will be another?" I asked Plush eagerly. I knew that a litter of guinea pigs could be as many as three or four or five. I was hoping for more.

Then, even as I spoke, another guinea pig emerged. "What a little pip-squeak she is," I exclaimed as I looked at our first daughter, who was smaller than her siblings. "Let's call her Pip."

Instantly a fourth head appeared. "It's Squeak!" I laughed. This fourth guinea pig pup was identical to Pip. We lay with the four damp infants cuddled around Plush as she proudly licked their fur.

Our first visitor was Lexi, of course.

"Look!" I shouted to him with delight and pride. "Have you ever seen anything more beautiful than these little babies?"

"*There is nothing more beautiful than a little nut, but . . . a big nut.*"

"Shame on you," I said. "Can you only

PUDGE   PERKY   PIP and SQUEAK

think of your stomach? Let me introduce you to Pudge, Perky, Pip, and Squeak."

"Sorry, sorry, sorry, sorry," said Lexi, looking ashamed of himself. "It just popped out of my mouth. It was one of my mother's sayings," he added, although I had already guessed as much.

"I like their names," Lexi said. "Squirrels aren't too clever about naming their offspring. Around here, we're all named for the city streets."

I nodded knowingly. In my months in the park, I'd met dozens and dozens of squirrels and they all had names like Seventy-seven and Fifty-two. And Lexi was named Lexington after an avenue.

"Well, I hope you remember the names of my children," I said. "You'll be seeing a lot of them."

"There *are* a lot of them," said Plush, looking around: "Pudge, Perky, Pip, and Squeak. Now we are truly a family."

✽   ✽   ✽

I can't explain it. Our four children were born within minutes of one another. They have the same set of parents and live in the same tree hole together. How could they be so different?

Pudge was the biggest and grew daily for he ate constantly. Even Lexi, who seems to be chewing or searching for a nut at all times, is impressed by Pudge's appetite. We need to watch Pudge carefully because he'll put anything in his mouth. Once, I overheard Plush scolding him when he was about to eat a buttercup, one of the plants that I warned her not to eat back when she first came to the park. Nevertheless, two days later Pudge came back into the hole and curled up in great pain. He had eaten one of these flowers and now he had a bad case of stomach cramps.

"A bad nut is worse than no nut," Lexi said when he saw Pudge in pain. But, thankfully, Pudge felt better within a few hours.

Pip and Squeak were just the opposite

of Pudge. They were the smallest of our offspring and kept busy with such energy and curiosity that they had to be reminded to eat. They poked their noses into every hole that they could find. They are small enough in size to get into and out of the tiniest crevices. "Watch your steps," I warned them.

"*Curiosity caught the squirrel*," said Lexi, who spent a lot of time checking on the progress of the babies.

"I won't be caught," replied Pip. "I'm not a squirrel. Besides, Pop," she said, turning to me, "I can run fast."

It's true. In addition to their lively, curious manner, Pip and Squeak move with more speed than our sons.

And then there was Perky. Both Plush and

I feared he was misnamed. Perky is not perky at all. Instead, he is timid, hardly ventures from our hole. He reminds me of Plush during her first hours in the park. But while Plush quickly outgrew her fears, Perky is just the opposite. Each day he seems to discover new things to be frightened of: the wind, leaves falling from the trees, squirrels, people walking by, dogs. Whatever he sees through the entrance to our hole seems to make him cringe with fear.

Why didn't my mother warn me about how hard it is to be a parent? It seems like I'm worried about my children all of the time.

"You don't have to worry about us, Pop," Pip said. "We can take care of ourselves."

I suppose I should believe her. I once read that in the early days of guinea pig history, all our ancestors lived outdoors in the Andes Mountains of South America, and the newborn of our species adapted to being surrounded by enemies at birth. Unlike other animals, such as baby rabbits, who are born blind, naked, and helpless, guinea pig babies are born with a warm coat of fur, open eyes, and a mouth full of teeth. Our newborns are able to go about alone and search for food, almost at once. Anyone watching Pudge, Pip, and Squeak could have seen that immediately.

Still, there were days when those children of ours caused us a great deal of anxiety. One evening at dusk they were playing near the hole. Gradually, however, Pip and Squeak made their way farther and farther from home.

"I hope they aren't lost," said Plush anxiously when she couldn't see or hear them nearby.

"Plush, I'm sure Pip and Squeak are fine. We must give them their independence. We want them to learn how to take care of themselves." I said those words confidently to ease Plush's worries. But the truth was that I was as nervous as she was about our young puppies.

As the evening got darker, I went looking for our daughters. I knew I could call on Lexi to help me, but like my children, I wanted to be independent. I walked many paws and was very relieved when I finally heard their voices.

"Look what we found!" exclaimed Squeak proudly.

Pip had a string in her mouth and it was attached to a large red balloon.

"We think it's a giant berry," said Squeak. Pip couldn't speak for fear of losing hold of the string, but she nodded her head in agreement.

I knew that what they'd found was not meant for eating. Did you sniff that before you grabbed for it? I wanted to say. But I kept my mouth shut. They had to learn some things for themselves. So I followed along with them as Pip pulled on the string and brought their find close to home. Of course, it would never fit inside our hole.

"What do you have?" asked Pudge eagerly when he saw his sisters. "Can I have a bite?" And then without waiting for their reply, Pudge sunk his teeth into the ball.

BANG!

A huge explosion sent poor Pudge rolling over backward. It certainly frightened the rest of us too. I'd known that what Pip found wasn't edible, but was only a plaything that some child had lost. And now all my children had learned the lesson, especially the always hungry Pudge.

The sound of that exploding ball terrified little Perky. He whimpered with fright for a long while afterward. And day after day, he insisted on remaining in our hole. Unlike his siblings, he always depended on Plush or me to bring him food. And since he was still drinking his mother's milk, he didn't need to go looking for water.

"Perky, come for a little walk with me," I had called when he was three days old. His brother and sisters were busy running around, but still he refused to venture out of the hole.

"The park is too big," Perky said.

"We won't walk through all of it. Just a few paws," I promised.

Perky shook his head. "I don't need a walk," he said.

"Come with us," Pip called to her brother. "We'll take care of you." She ran over and licked his head affectionately.

But Perky wouldn't budge. He moved deeper into our hole and curled up into a ball. "Leave me alone," he said.

It would have been easy to do that. It was enough of an effort watching the antics of our three other pups. But Plush and I knew that we had to encourage Perky to go outside. What we didn't know was how to do it. We had a real problem on our paws.

CHAPTER NINE

Running Away from Winter

And then we had another problem. One morning soon after the full hunter's moon, when our children were almost five weeks old, we woke to discover that the air was colder than usual and a fine covering of white was on the ground. I stepped out onto it carefully and noticed that the ground was very cold. When I turned to look back toward the hole, I discovered that I'd left a series of paw prints behind me.

Pip and Squeak came out of the hole and jumped about on the cold ground. They were fascinated by the tracks that they made. Pudge came out, but, as usual, he was more interested in finding something to put inside his stomach.

By the time Lexi jumped down to give us his morning greeting, the white was almost gone.

"How did you like your first snow?" he called to us.

"Was that snow?" Plush asked in amazement. "I thought snow was thick and deep and icy cold."

"If that was snow, we've nothing to be afraid of," I said, thinking of the soft wet covering that had disappeared so quickly. It was nothing like the cloudlike stuff I'd seen in the magazine photos.

"Snow is light and snow is heavy," said Lexi. "Snow is dry and snow is wet. Snow is beautiful and snow is dangerous. This morning we had a teasing snow. It fools you into thinking that winter will be easy. But it rarely is. Beware of winter, my friends."

That was a long speech from Lexi and his final words were as chilling as the air around us. Plush and I looked at each other. If what Lexi said was true, our days in our cozy hole were numbered.

"Is this winter?" I asked.

"No. It's still autumn. And we will probably even have two or three days of false summer when the air becomes very hot once again. But winter is on its way. It's almost here."

I nodded. Every day for the past few weeks I'd seen birds flying overhead and calling out their farewells to us. "We'll be back in the spring," the robins chirped. Just the day before I'd seen an enormous **V** formation of Canada geese on their way south too. We could see that many of the animals were getting ready for winter. Only the pigeons and the squirrels were staying put.

It was time for us guinea pigs to move to our planned winter quarters.

Except that we had a problem. It took Plush and me well over two hours to make the long trek to the zoo. This wouldn't be a problem for Pip and Squeak. They'd be thrilled by the chance to go off exploring new areas. Pudge too would welcome a chance to find new tidbits as we traveled to the southern end of the park. But how were we going to get Perky to make the journey. His short legs had never gone very far. He didn't have the stamina or strength of his siblings. The trip would be long and dangerous for him.

Lexi seemed to read my thoughts. "I could give Perky a ride over to the zoo," he offered.

"Oh, Lexi," I said with relief, "would you do that? It would be wonderful."

"No, no, no!" shrieked Perky when he

heard our plan. "He goes too fast and too high. What if I fall off? I would break all of my bones!"

"If you hold on to my fur tightly, you'll be fine," Lexi told our pup.

"Suppose my paw slips?" he asked. "No, no, no. I can't do it." He shuddered at the thought.

"What if we make the trip in two parts?" I suggested. "We could go halfway one day and the rest the next day. I'm sure I can find a hole where we can camp overnight."

"Perhaps that's the best way," Plush conceded. She turned to Lexi. "Thank you very much for your generous offer," she said. "Perky is just too timid to take a ride with you."

"I'd love a ride," said Pudge, swallowing the seeds he'd been chewing on.

"You're much too heavy for poor Lexi to carry," I retorted at once. "And the walk to the zoo will be good for you. You won't get much exercise during the winter when we're hiding in the rain forest."

"We'll get our exercise at night after the zoo closes," Plush reminded me.

Plush and I talked over our plans. We decided we would leave together the next morning. Lexi said he'd look for us from time to time. If he wasn't carrying Perky, he could travel along the tree branches and see if there were any problems ahead.

CHAPTER TEN

An Unusual Journey

The next morning we started out. It was a cool and cloudy day that could easily become a rainy one. But for now, it was a perfect day for travel. There are always fewer people about when the sun isn't shining.

I led the way, with Pudge, Pip, and Squeak following close behind. In the rear came Plush and Perky side by side. Plush had not given Perky any seeds for breakfast and only the smallest swallow of milk. "We'll find food along the way," she promised him, hoping his hunger would keep him moving. She had to urge Perky every step of the way.

"That's it. Good. Good. Come on, another step. Another. Another."

Meanwhile, I had to keep busy watching after our other offspring. Each one went off in a different direction pursuing a leaf or a seed or a nut that they saw. "Stick close together," I reminded them over and over. "Be ready to hide if necessary."

I don't know who had the more difficult job, Plush or me. Often I'd hear Perky crying out in alarm. At first I ran back every time. But after the fourth or fifth episode, I realized that he was just frightened by things like a leaf fluttering to the ground or his foot accidentally kicking a small pebble. He was not in any danger at all, so I hurried to catch up with my three other children who had gone ahead.

"This is fun," Pip called to me. Her eyes were shining with delight.

We went on a bit longer before I realized that I was no longer hearing any sounds coming from Plush or Perky. That couldn't be a good sign. "Pups, wait here. Don't go any farther until I return," I instructed Pudge, Pip, and Squeak. Then I retraced my steps looking for the others.

"Here we are," Plush called out to me from under a bush. "We had to stop. Perky can't go any farther. He's twisted his paw."

"Then let him ride on Lexi," I said impatiently. I loved my son, but I was concerned about the safety of my whole family. We couldn't risk being exposed to the cold weather and snow. Even the bush we were resting under wasn't the good hiding place it would have been a moon ago. Many of its leaves had already fallen off.

"Perky won't do it," said Plush. Then she whispered so Perky wouldn't hear. "And though I admire Lexi, I'd be afraid too. He might start off slowly, but the chances are he'd suddenly see one of his cousins and start chasing after him. That's the way squirrels are. They aren't meant to carry others around."

"Oh, dear," I said, suddenly remembering

my other responsibility. "Now I've got to find the other pups. Wait here. I'll bring them back and then we'll talk this over."

It was easier said than done. I found Pudge close to where I'd left him. He was chewing on a pinecone and savoring each of its seeds. "Where are Pip and Squeak?" I asked him.

"Who?" he asked, as if he'd never heard those names before.

"Your sisters, that's who. Where are they?"

"Oh. I don't know. Around, I guess," said Pudge, removing another seed from the pinecone.

"Stay here," I told him, but it was quite unnecessary. There were enough seeds to keep him busy for a long while.

I rushed along the path stopping from

time to time to listen. The problem was that the wind blowing through the leaves sounded similar to two guinea pigs running through the dried grass. I stopped to catch my breath. Perhaps Lexi was smart not to get involved with the responsibilities of parent-hood. But I couldn't turn off my concern. I worried that a dog had caught my children and I continued on my search. Suddenly I heard a strange whirring noise. Instinctively, I crouched low while I looked around. There before me was a large shoe with wheels attached. It moved closer and I backed away.

I'd seen such shoes before. Lexi told me they were called *roller skates*. Usually they were seen in pairs and a human would be wearing them. But this one roller skate was unat-tached to anything.

"Hi, Pop," a voice called to me. "Look what we found. It was under a park bench."

"What do you think you're doing?" I exclaimed to Pip, who came forward from the other side of the roller skate. "Why are you playing in full view where anyone could see you?"

"There's no one around today," Pip said.

"Where's Squeak now?" I asked.

"Here I am, Pop," my younger daughter said, crawling out from inside the shoe. I hadn't even noticed her.

"Well, come along at once, both of you.

We have to go back to your mother and Perky. We have a big journey ahead of us. There's no time to play," I scolded them.

So there we were, Plush and I and our four offspring. We hadn't gotten very far from our hole and it didn't seem as if we'd ever make it to the rain forest. We huddled together under a bush for a midmorning rest.

While the others slept, I worried about the situation and considered our options:

1. We could return home and brave out the winter.
2. I could return home with Perky while Plush and the other pups spend the winter in the rain forest.
3. Or, I could force Perky to ride on Lexi.

The third choice seemed to be the best. But I knew I had to reject it. Plush was absolutely right. Lexi was bound to begin climbing trees and leaping on branches even if he was carrying my little Perky. Squirrels just behave that way. It's their nature. But if we didn't get to the rain forest, I was afraid we'd be doomed.

No warmth, no cheerfulness, no healthful ease,
No comfortable feel in any member—

Member. That was a funny word for "limb," I thought, dozing off, thinking of paws and hands and tails and feet. Feet! Suddenly I woke with a start. The solution to our problem had come to me. We could use the skate to get to the rain forest. Perky could ride in it. That is, if we could convince him to get inside.

Luckily, the skate was still where Pip and Squeak had left it. With some effort, I managed to move the skate along the bumpy ground toward where my family still lay sleeping. I woke everyone up and explained my new plan. There was much chatter among them when they heard what I had to say.

"What fun you're going to have," Squeak shouted to Perky. He didn't look so sure of that.

Plush and I had to help Perky climb inside the shoe part of the skate. As always he was reluctant to try a new experience, and I had to give him a few hard pushes to get him moving. Once inside the skate, he curled himself into a ball.

"Don't you want to look out?" Pip called to her brother. "You won't be able to see where you're going."

Perky lifted his head for a moment. "I don't want to see," he replied.

"I don't care if you look or not," I said. "The important thing is that now you'll be moving at a better speed." Then I took the laces that hung down from the skate in my mouth and used them to pull the skate along. It was harder than ever to move the skate now that it had the weight of Perky added to it. It occurred to me that if I went on the cement path, instead of traveling in the grass as I usually did, the skate would roll with much greater ease.

Now there was a new problem. Out on the walkway, I was visible to any passersby. It was a piece of luck that the cool, damp weather of the day did not encourage many people to use the park. There were no mothers or nannies pushing carriages. Only a few solitary individuals were walking their dogs or strolling through the park. So from time to time as I saw someone, I had to pull the skate and veer off the path and into a bush to avoid a human I saw coming toward us. It was quite exhausting.

After a time, Perky stuck his head out. "This is fun!" he exclaimed. I don't believe my son had ever in his life found anything to be fun before.

So I kept on going. Perky's change of heart gave me new strength. I panted when there was a steep incline on the sidewalk, but I kept on pulling. Suddenly the incline ended and the sidewalk sloped downhill. What a relief. I dropped the shoelace and stopped to catch my breath. I turned and waved to Plush who was a short distance away with our other children. Suddenly her face filled with horror and she screamed out to me.

"PeeWee! Look at the skate!"

I looked back at the skate and saw that it had started to roll down the hill on its own. I ran after it, trying to grab the shoelace, and finally I caught it by its tip. I held on as tightly as I could, but the skate was moving so fast that it lifted my feet off the ground.

Suddenly the shoelace was pulled out of my mouth and I landed on the cement path with a thud. A moment later I sat up, dazed, and then horrified, as I saw that the skate was rolling downhill faster than ever with poor little Perky trapped inside.

CHAPTER ELEVEN

Journey's End

"Stop! Stop!" I shouted.

But Perky couldn't and the skate wouldn't.

Ignoring my bruises, I raced down the hill after the runaway skate.

Plush, Pudge, Pip, and Squeak came running and calling out behind me. But we discovered that guinea pigs are no match for a roller skate.

Finally the wild skate slowed down and

fell over on its side as it veered off the walk-way. I rushed toward it terrified of what I would find inside. Could Perky have survived such a tumble?

And then I saw his little head peeking out of the skate. "Hi, Pop," he shouted cheerfully. "That was great. Can we do it again?"

"Great?" I sputtered, thinking of how the skate had run me down and left me so frightened regarding Perky's fate. And what about my sore body?

"It was like flying," Perky said. "I felt like I was a bird!"

"You're a guinea pig," I said. "Why do you want to feel like a bird?" But then I laughed. Perky was safe, unharmed, and happy. And I was happy too.

We decided it was high time for a little rest.

"Lucky you," said Pudge, looking at Perky still inside the shoe. "You're getting a ride all the way to our new home. It's not fair."

I was about to defend Perky. After all, he had twisted his paw earlier. But to my surprise, Perky spoke up. "You can have a turn, Pudge," he offered. And with that, he climbed out of the shoe without any assistance and walked alongside of it with Pip and Squeak when our rest period was over. The twisted paw seemed just fine. Perhaps Perky hadn't really twisted it at all.

Plush and I looked at each other with amazement. What had happened to change our timid son? Was it the first real dose of good fresh air in his lungs? Was it the fact that the park was almost empty of humans and dogs that cold, cloudy day? I don't know the answer. But it was a joy to watch all of our children chattering happily, running, and riding in the skate. Each had a turn inside. Even Plush.

"Pop. You should have a turn too," said Pudge.

"Well, I don't mind if I do," I replied. "But you'll have to work to pull me. This skate won't move by itself."

Twice during our journey we saw Lexi. His eyes nearly popped out of his head the first time he saw the skate.

"PeeWee, you're even smarter than I ever guessed," he told me. "*A good head is better than two tails.*"

He'd told me that once before, but repetition didn't make those words any less satisfying.

We arrived at the zoo in the late afternoon. With great regret we abandoned the skate. I pushed it under a bush and tried to cover it with leaves. I doubted it would remain there all winter long. But having seen Perky actually being perky for the first time in his life, I felt we would be able to manage to return to our home when the weather turned warm again, even if we didn't have the skate to transport us.

Thankfully, all of us, even Pudge, were small enough to slip under the door of the rain forest without waiting for a human to open it. Inside, we stood savoring the warmth and good smells around us. I knew in a few days the pups would be running all over this place. There was much to explore and many new animals to befriend. And best of all, we would be safe from the winter.

I settled my family in a hollow log and then slipped outdoors again. As I had hoped, there was Lexi waiting at the entrance.

"So you made it here," he said.

"Yes. I'm proud of the pups. They all pulled together," I reported.

"Well, winter is a long time. I'm going to miss you," Lexi said to me.

"And I'll miss you," I replied. "But I hope you'll come by from time to time. You can tell me what's going on in the rest of the park."

"I will. I will," said Lexi. "*A nut is good but a good friend is better.*"

"Thanks, pal," I said. "That's one of the best sayings your mother ever taught you."

Lexi scratched himself and winked at me. "That's one saying my mother never knew. I made it up myself," Lexi responded.

We parted and I went back inside. A small bat was flying around in the dark and I introduced myself.

"Do you eat insects?" he asked me.

"No," I said, wondering if he was about to offer me one.

"Good, good," the bat replied. "In that case, welcome to the rain forest."

"Thanks," I said to my first new friend in this area. Obviously, he was not as generous as my pal Lexi.

I returned to my family. They were all cuddled around one another inside the hollow log and already fast asleep. It had been a long and difficult day. No wonder they were all tired. I could hardly keep my eyes open either.

As I moved close to Plush and all our

little pups, I thought of Thomas Hood's poem. New and happier words came to me replacing the words I'd memorized.

> *No ice—no snow!*
> *No winds that blow!*
> *No chill—no shock—*
> *No ground like rock.*
> *Just snug and warm—*
> *We're safe from harm,*
> *November, in the rain forest!*

Goodness, I thought to myself, I've become a poet too. I wondered if I could create some other poems during the long winter ahead. It could be a new activity as I watched my family grow and develop.

Plush turned over in her sleep and let out

a series of soft sounds. I recognized them as a melody from one of the operas we had heard during the summer. She was dreaming of her favorite music. Soon I'd be asleep and dreaming happy dreams too. What more could I wish for?

About the Author and Illustrator

Johanna Hurwitz was born and raised in New York City. A former children's librarian, she is now the award-winning author of many popular books for young readers, including *PeeWee's Tale*; *Lexi's Tale*; *Oh No, Noah!*; *Class Clown*; *Rip-Roaring Russell*; and *Baseball Fever*. The recipient of a number of child-chosen state awards, she visits schools around the country to speak to students, teachers and parents about reading and writing. She lives in both Great Neck, New York, and Wilmington, Vermont.

Patience Brewster has illustrated more than thirty books, including *Bear's Christmas Surprise* by Elizabeth Winthrop and *Queen of May* by Steven Kroll. She lives in Skaneateles, New York.